For Jack, Ellie, Lloyd and Lewis – J.P

First edition for the United States and Canada published in 2005 by
Barron's Educational Series, Inc.

First published by Hodder Children's Books, a division of
Hodder Headline Limited, 338 Euston Road, London NW1 3BH

Copyright © John Prater 2004

All inquiries should be addressed to:
Barron's Educational Series, Inc.
250 Wireless Boulevard
Hauppauge, New York 11788
http://www.barronseduc.com

Library of Congress Catalog Card No.: 2004105595
International Standard Book No.: 0-7641-5815-5

Printed in China

There's Always One!

John Prater

BARRON'S

It was a hot summer's day – perfect for a trip to the beach.
Dad counted the bunnies.

"One, two, three, four, five, six, seven, eight, nine, ten, eleven..."

Jacob was missing!

"There's always one," said Mom.

"Jacob!"

Jacob came clattering down the stairs.
"Sorry," he gasped. "Just packing!"
Mom laughed. "Do you really need
all of that?"

"All of what?" said Jacob.

When they arrived at the beach, everyone was very excited. They settled in a sheltered spot and started to change.

But not Jacob!

"There's always one!" sighed Dad.

He gave Jacob a big rubber ring. **"Now** you can swim," he said.

But one wasn't enough for Jacob!

And two was too many!

"There's always one," laughed Dad, again.

"Come on, you two," shouted Mom. **"Let's dig!"**

Jacob built a sand castle.
It was big and tall and it had a moat.

Sadly,   **it didn't last**

very long.

"There's always one!" sighed Mom. "Come and have some lunch."

But Jacob wasn't hungry.

Dad was cross.

"There's always one," he said.
"Eat up quietly.
Then it's rest time!"

But Jacob wasn't tired.
"Sleeping is boring,"
he sighed.
"I want to go
exploring!"

So, when the others were all fast asleep,
off he went.
I won't go far, he thought.

Some time later, the others awoke.
Something was different...
Someone had taken away the beach.
There was water everywhere.

They were stuck!

HELP!

Mom started to count:

"One, two, three, four, five, six, seven, eight, nine, ten, eleven...

Oh no!"
she shouted.

"Behind you,"
cried a little voice.

Jacob had found a cave.
"Look, there's daylight,"
he called. "Follow me!"

"Phew," said Dad. "That was close."
"It was," laughed Mom, "we nearly
had to swim back."

"But there's always one, isn't there!

Well done, Jacob!"